James and the Ancient Woodland Creatures.

Billie Potter

ISBN:
ISBN-13: 9781687132802

DEDICATION

To all those who love nature.

ACKNOWLEDGMENTS

To Mother Nature, whom we should
Look after, for the generations to come.

n an ancient forest quite near to where you live are some creatures that you will never have heard of.

In fact no one has ever heard of them, no one has ever seen them and nobody knows anything about them.

So why is this, and how is it that you are now about to read about them?

———

They have been here, near you, for as long as us humans have been around. In fact, it could be that some time, a long time ago, they were related to us.

They are very like us in so many ways. They look a lot like us, they live a lot like us and they behave a lot like us, just not quite like us.

One of the differences, and also one of the reasons that they don't want us to know that they exist, is that they've watched us doing things like chasing and killing wild animals just for sport, just for our own fun. They have seen us capturing animals and putting them in cages or in chains or on leads just so that we can look at them, just for our own pleasure. They don't do that sort of thing and they don't like it.

These creatures are afraid that if we humans were to discover them we might do the same to them and that would be horrible, terrible, disastrous.

———————

So, why have you never seen them? You have probably been into the woods or a forest or even a little coppice, and they are there, right in front of you.

The thing is that they have lived in these tree areas for ever, well, for as long as we humans have lived in the open spaces, as long as we have lived in caves or in dens or houses of one sort or another.

In all of that time they have become 'at one' with the trees and the trees have accepted them as part of their family.

When you or I or your friends and family, in fact any and all of we humans are not in the forest or wooded area these creatures that are so like us play openly amongst the trees and bushes. They gather their food there and build their homes there, they talk to each other

3

and do all sorts of things that we do in our daily lives.
BUT, whenever one of us humans goes anywhere near them they scatter and disappear.
They really are frightened of us.
Each one of them chooses a tree to go to and they stand and lean into their chosen tree.

The trees feel that these creatures are such a part of them that they sort of absorb them, they sort of wrap themselves around these creatures, making them part of the tree and they become almost invisible to us humans.

If you look really closely, maybe squint your eyes a little, you can sometimes make out the shape of one of these creatures. Sometimes you can almost see a face in the tree trunk, they are there.

Hundreds and hundreds and hundreds of years ago these ancient forests covered almost all of the land and we humans only had a little bit of open space in which we lived.

Over time, over many hundreds of years we have gradually chopped the trees down to make space so that we can grow crops or graze our sheep and cattle. We have also used the trees to build our homes and ship's, or just used the wood to burn on our fires. We have chopped so many trees down that now there is not much forest area left, not much left for all of the forest creatures to live in.

———

You are now going to meet one of the forest creatures. This one is called 'Zugduf'. It's not the sort of name that you will be used to, but then why would you, you're not one of these creatures, these 'tree people'. Neither will you be able to speak their language or understand what they say. They can understand what you say however because they are there in the forest or woods whenever you or I go into them, and they listen to what we are saying.

———

Zugduf is just an ordinary tree person, no different to any other.

Zugduf, like all the others is very worried about the ancient forest where they live.

Like all of the country's forests, the one that Zugduf's family and all their friends live in has gradually been chopped down until there is not much of it left, and they are all squeezed into a very small area. Worse still is that a couple of years ago we humans cut their forest in half when we cleared a way through it so that some big lorries could get to a factory quicker and easier.

This was bad for Zugduf and the family because it cut them off from many of their friends and family. Zugduf and the other tree people do not like going out into the open or crossing open spaces, so they weren't able to see their friends or some of their family any more.

NOW things were about to get even worse for Zugduf's family and friends, in fact for all of the forest creatures because we humans were about to cut down a whole lot more of their forest so that we could build more factories and houses.

―――――

The tree people decided to have a meeting about the forthcoming doom and at that meeting it was decided that someone should try to tell their family and friends in the other part of the ancient forest, the bit that had been cut off from them, about what was going to happen, and to see if anyone could think of a way to rescue the situation and all of them.
Eventually, after a lot of talking Zugduf volunteered to try to cross the open space between the two

bits of ancient forest to tell the others what was happening.

———

Zugduf thought for a very long time because of being frightened at having to cross the open space and he worried about being caught by a human and wondered what they might do if that happened.
Zugduf decided that the best time to go would be just as it began to get dark. It was always about this time that the humans seemed to disappear into their homes, so with a bit of luck that is when Zugduf would have the best chance of getting to the other part of the ancient forest.

———

It was just as the daylight was fading that Zugduf started to cross the open space and was almost halfway to the other bit of the ancient forest when the cry and sobbing of a human child caused an abrupt halt. Zugduf froze for a moment hoping that no one had seen this creature from the forest. The sobbing continued and was so very sad that Zugduf peered into a shallow dip where it was coming from.

Laying at the bottom of the dip was a human child, this frightened Zugduf and normally any forest creature would have run away as fast and as far as they could, but the cry and the sobbing was so sad, so upsetting, that Zugduf didn't feel able to leave this human child there on his own.

———

Zugduf slowly approached the human child and gingerly held out a hand to comfort it.

It soon became clear that this human child had fallen and had badly hurt himself. In fact he had hurt himself so badly that he couldn't stand up and walk, it even hurt just to move.

Zugduf gently talked to this human child in human language, something that Zugduf had learned by listening to all the humans that went into the ancient forest, and the boy told Zugduf that his name was James and that he lived not far from where they were.

James asked Zugduf to help him get home.

Zugduf was not at all happy to help James return home because humans might do all kinds of bad things if they captured a forest creature.

After a lot of pleading from James, Zugduf lifted him up and carried him towards his home. All the while Zugduf was very worried about what might happen, but James needed help otherwise he might be left out alone all night.
Eventually the two of them got to the door of the cottage where James lived and Zugduf gently put James down on the door step.

Before Zugduf could get away the door opened, it opened surprisingly quickly, startling Zugduf, and in fear the forest creature run to the nearest tree which was a little apple tree in the garden, and Zugduf tried to disappear into it.

Had the apple tree been bigger Zugduf would have succeeded, but it wasn't, so bits of Zugduf hung out for all to see.

At first James' parents were more
interested in their son and so
almost didn't see Zugduf's attempt
to hide. Zugduf might even have got
away with it had James not pointed
and told his parents of how he had
rescued him and carried him home.
To Zugduf's surprise James'
parents were nice people, and
although they thought it very odd

that Zugduf was trying to blend in with their apple tree, they greeted this forest creature and thanked him for saving their son.

———

Zugduf retreated back to his ancient forest after this encounter and decided that it was so frightening that going into the open should never happen again.

It was some weeks later that James visited the ancient forest again. All of the forest creatures had hidden in their favourite trees, blending into the tree trunks and then waiting for the human, James, to leave the forest so that they could continue with their lives. James sat down at the foot of one of the trees, not just any tree but the one that Zugduf used to hide in.

Somehow James seemed to feel, to know, that this is where Zugduf would be, and he sat there and started to talk, as if to himself, because there were no other humans around, but in fact he was talking to Zugduf. He told Zugduf how grateful his parents were and how grateful he was that Zugduf had helped him. James said that he was now much better, but that he had been really badly injured and might have died had it not been for Zugduf.

James talked and talked, he seemed to know that Zugduf was a different creature and that Zugduf was afraid, and that it must have been a very brave act to carry a human all the way to a human's house.

James said that he would never forget Zugduf's kindness and hoped that one day he might be able to help the forest creatures in some way.

———

James was just about to stand up and leave the forest when Zugduf's arm came from out of the tree trunk and gently placed a hand on James' shoulder.
James was so happy that Zugduf had done this that he gave the tree trunk a really big hug.

James looked into Zugduf's eyes and asked him what he was so afraid of and Zugduf told him about what the humans did to the tree people, that is Zugduf's people, and to the forest and all the creatures in the ancient forest.

Zugduf also told James about the plans to cut down more of their trees and about how that would devastate so many of the various creatures that live in the forest. James eventually left the forest to go home in a very sad mood, a very sad mood indeed.

———

At home James told his mum and dad about the plans to cut down a lot of the forest and he asked if there was anything that could be done to stop it.

They said that unfortunately men who thought that they could make money out of it would be very difficult to stop, and that sort of person didn't really care about others.

James and his parents talked for ages about the forest but could not think of any way that would stop the forest from being destroyed.

———

It was a few days later that James went back to sit at the base of his favourite tree, the one where Zugduf blended into.

There was a tear in James' eye as he told Zugduf what his mum and dad had said, and Zugduf let a few tears fall as well.

James decided that he had to do something to help his friend. He started by writing to the builders who were going to cut the trees down so that they could build houses. Then he wrote to the local politicians and then to the local newspapers to try to get them to somehow stop the forests destruction.

Nothing seemed to work so James then started to find pieces of cardboard and bits of wood to paint on. He wrote things like "save our trees" and "stop cutting our trees down" and "don't kill our forest creatures".

James took the signs that he had painted and put them up all over the place. He nailed some to the trees at the edge of the forest, and although it hurt the trees when he bashed the nails into them, they didn't mind too much because they knew that he was trying to help them.

Nobody seemed to take any notice of anything that James did, it seemed that he had failed to help his friend.

Zugduf told James how sad it would be because some of the creatures that live in the forest would be gone forever when the trees were cut down as there was nowhere else that they could live, nowhere else they could go to.

That saddened James and he asked Zugduf to show him these creatures so that he would at least have seen them before they disappeared for ever. So Zugduf took James to the part of the forest where these creatures lived.
There were several different creatures in particular that had become very rare in recent years, Zugduf didn't know what name

humans would give them so James just had to look and make his own mind up.

One of the creatures was a bit like a grass hopper, but only seemed to appear about every eight years or so, another was like a little bee or wasp but it wasn't one of those and a third creature flew but it didn't have wings or feathers like the birds which James knew.

James thanked Zugduf for showing him these animals before he and Zugduf each went back to their homes.

————

It was over tea that night that James told his mum and dad about the creatures that he had seen in the forest and about how they would die out when all of the trees were cut down.

James described what these creatures looked like and together with his parents they tried to find pictures of them in some books which they had.

————

The next day James took his parents into the woods and to where he had seen the creatures that Zugduf had shown him.
It was a few days later, after James' parents had made a few phone calls, that some other humans arrived to look at what James had discovered.

————

Very soon there were protesters, humans, all around the edges of the ancient forest, not going into it, but staying just outside it. They were doing everything they could to make sure that the ancient forest was left alone, not cut down.

The national newspapers were quick to follow, this was becoming a big story and they were all trying to get the biggest headlines, and so, it wasn't too long before the politicians arrived, promising to do something to stop the destruction of this special ancient forest.

———

What Zugduf had shown James, what James had shown his parents and what they had shown some experts were three creatures that were rare and were on the list of endangered animals and so should be protected, and the way to protect them was to protect where they live.

It didn't take long for the protection orders to be taken out for these ancient woods.
It was also decided that the two ancient woods that used to be just one, which had been cut in two, should be restored, so new trees would be planted between them and the track would be closed so that the forest creatures would be able to travel around the whole of the ancient woodlands.

————

As the years passed James often went quietly and on his own into the ancient forest. He would sit leaning against his favourite tree and chat away to it, and to his friend Zugduf.

He often felt the gentle hand of Zugduf on his shoulder, and these were the happiest moments of his life.
James never told anyone else about Zugduf and the tree people, and neither must you.

Appendix.

The creature that looked like a wasp was really a fly, it was called a Golden Hoverfly, the grasshopper looking one was a cicada which apparently stayed underground for something like eight years as it grew and developed into it's adult state and the flying creature was a bat, it was a rare bat called a Bechsteins Bat and only lived in these forests.

Printed in Great Britain
by Amazon

73193022R00021